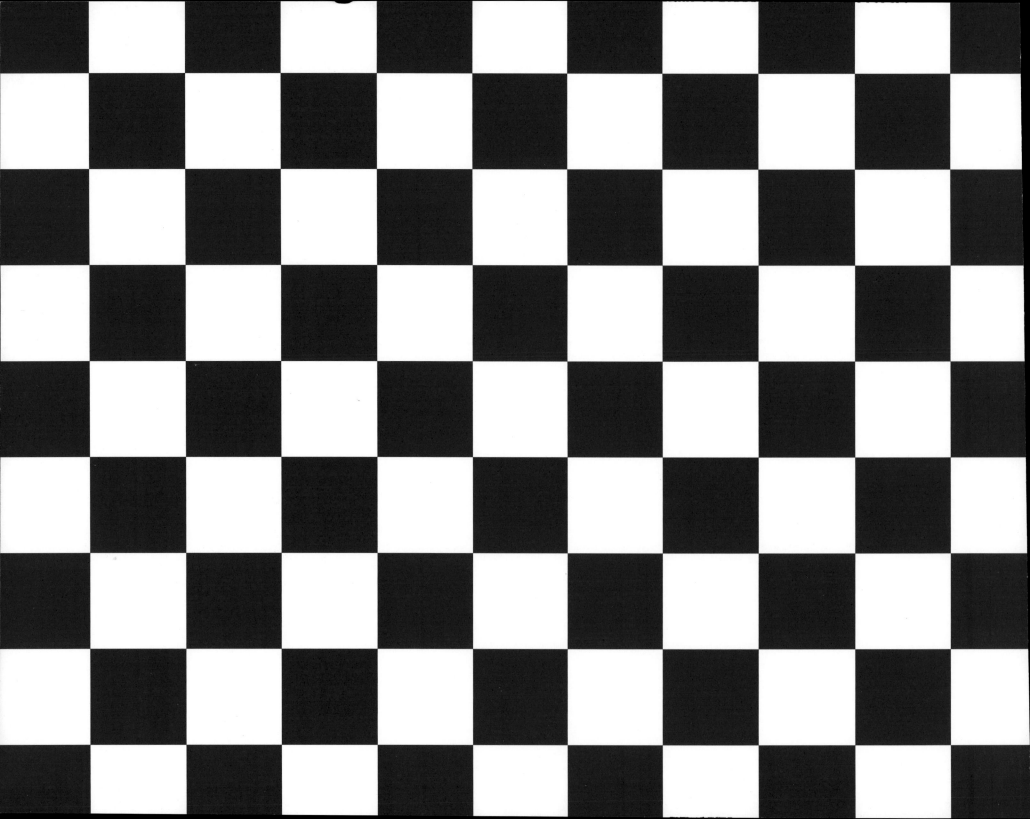

SPEED

Nathan Clement

BOYDS MILLS PRESS

AN IMPRINT OF HIGHLIGHTS

Honesdale, Pennsylvania

For Winnie, and dinner crashing

Many thanks to the two Tims: Tim Biddle and Tim Noblitt, for sharing their racing knowledge

Text and illustrations copyright © 2013 by Nathan Clement

Boyds Mills Press, Inc.
815 Church Street
Honesdale, Pennsylvania 18431
Printed in China
ISBN: 978-1-59078-937-7
Library of Congress Control Number: 2012945818

First edition
The text of this book is set in Rockwell.
The pictures in this book are computer-rendered. Just as an artist may use oil paint, Nathan uses color
fills and blends within shapes to create his artwork. Everything he makes begins as pencil drawings
before the computer magic can ever happen.

10 9 8 7 6 5 4 3 1

Common Stock-Car Racing Flags

Start or restart:
Track is clear.

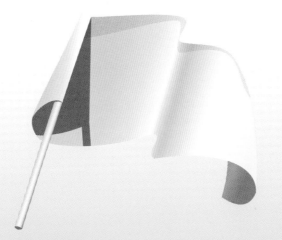

Caution:
Track is not clear.
Stay in position.

Stop:
Track is unsafe.

Problem or penalty:
Come into the pits.

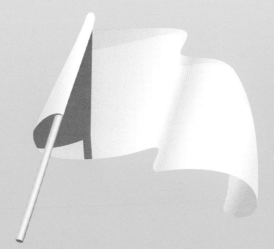

Final lap:
Only one lap left in the race.

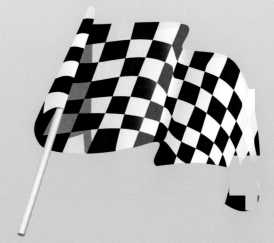

Finish:
Race is over.

Rows and rows of cars. The green flag is ready. "Ladies and gentlemen, start—your—engines!" *ROAR!*

Revved-up cars rumble behind the pace car.

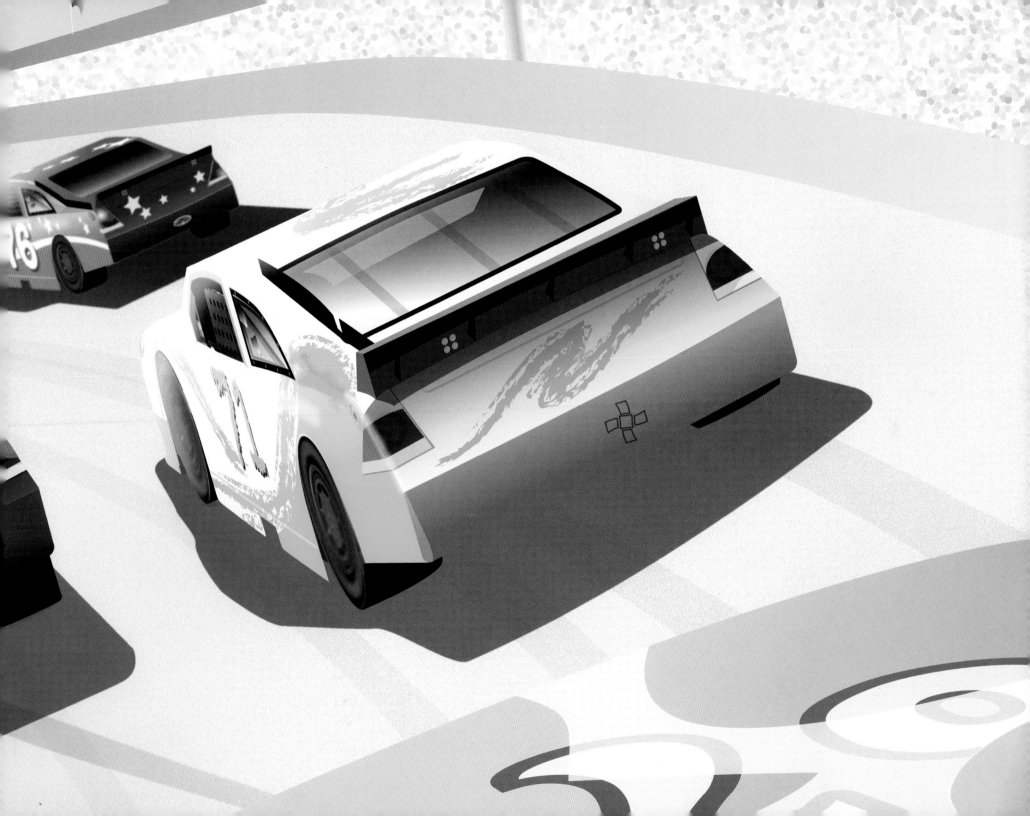

One lap, two laps, three laps.
The green flag rips across the sky.
VROOM!

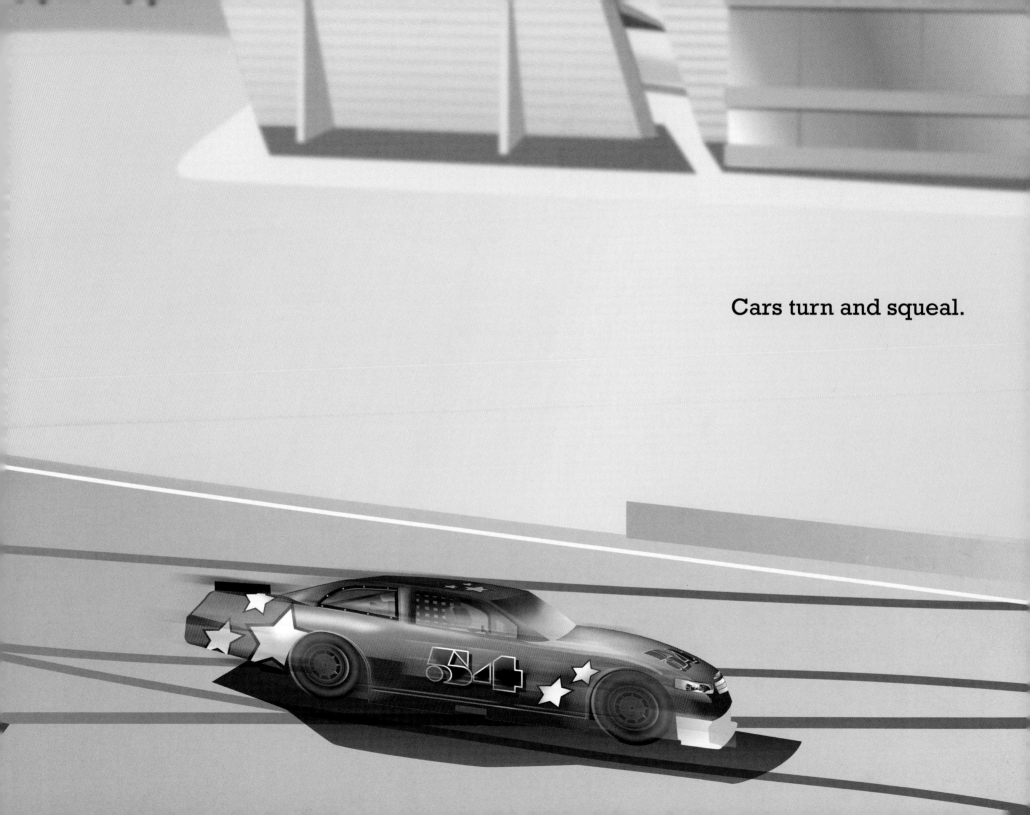

Cars turn and squeal.

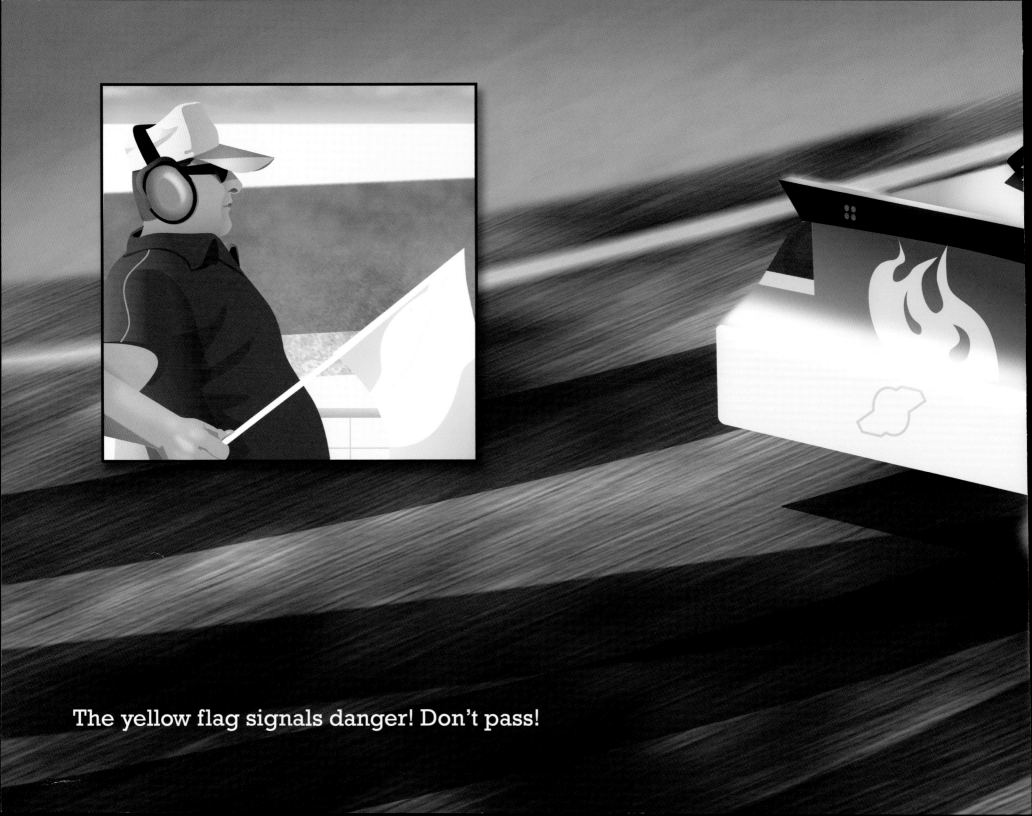

The yellow flag signals danger! Don't pass!

The pack of cars circles the track behind the pace car.

Race cars hit the pits.

Refuel. Jack up. Change tires.

The green flag cracks the air.
It's pedal to the metal.

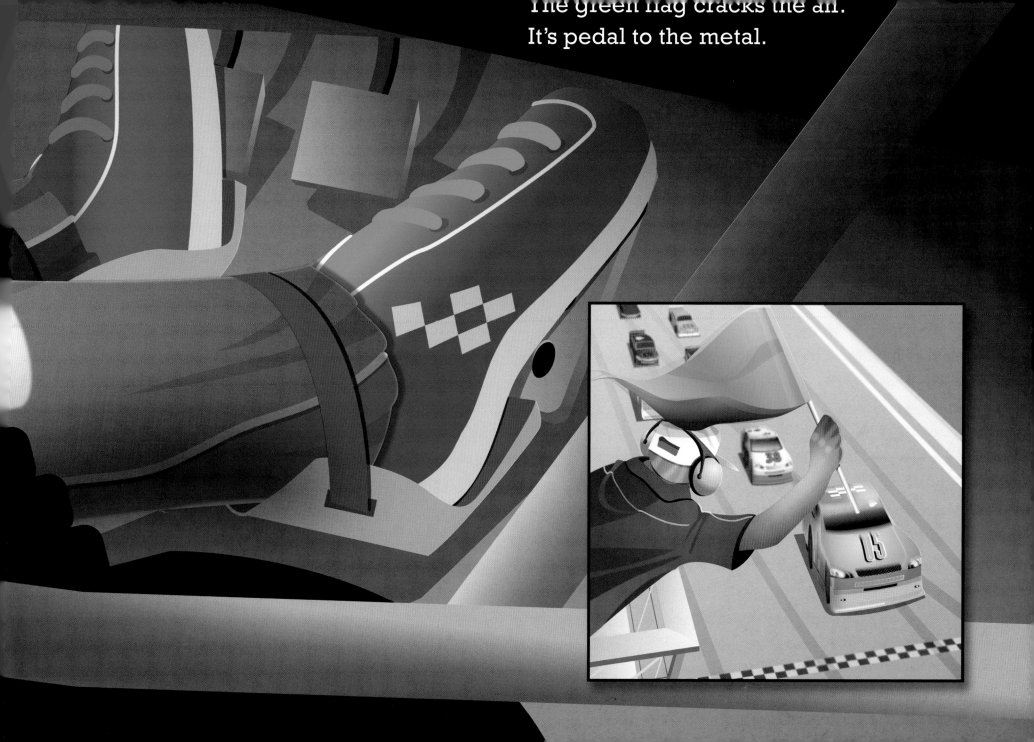

Car 53 and Car 19 bump, spin, smash and crash!
The red flag waves. Stop the race!

Crews clear metal, tire rubber, and oil.
The track is now safe.

The green flag flies over the stand!

Cars race until the white flag waves. Last lap!

Car 42 bursts across the finish line as the checkered flag flaps.

"The winner! Yay! Line up.
The next race is about to begin!"

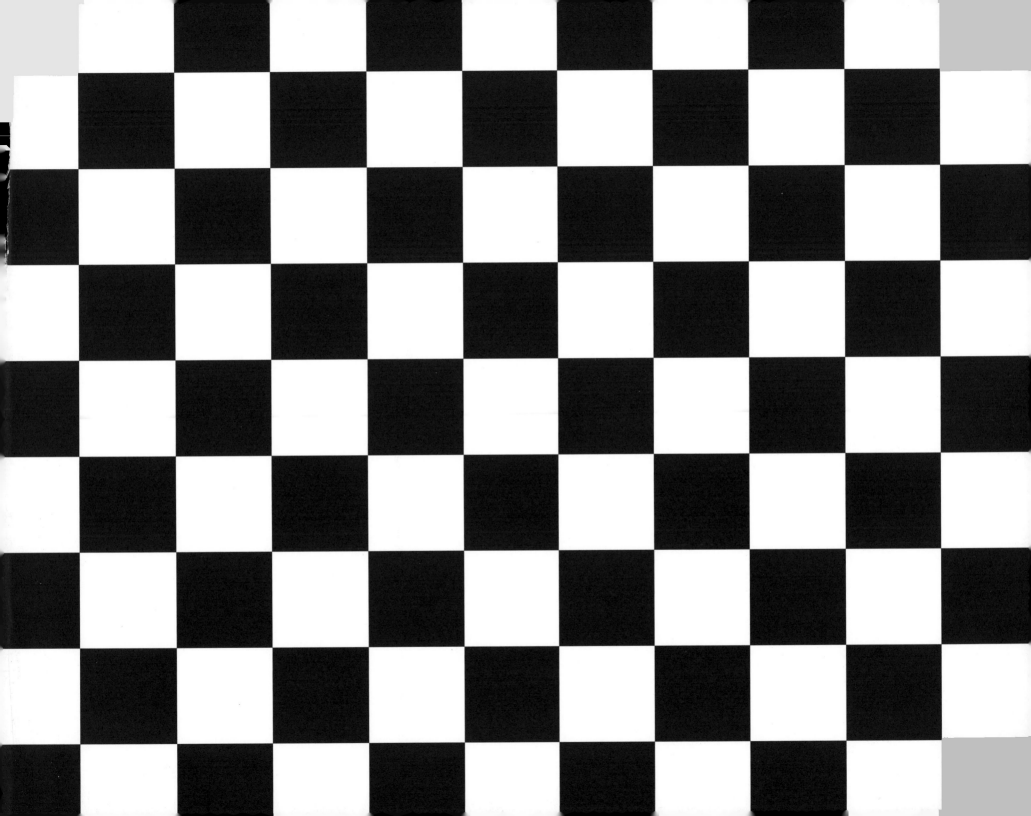